Dylan Discovers Yoga

First edition: December 2022

ISBN: 979-8-9874535-0-6

To Camille and Simone,

May you feel and know how deeply loved
you are.

And to children of all ages,

May we be brave enough to try.

Dylan the tuxedo cat was very curious. He liked to learn.

One afternoon, Dylan went for a walk and ran into his friend Mittens.

"I'm going to a yoga class. Do you want to come along?" Mittens asked.

Dylan had never heard of yoga before. "What is yoga?" he asked.

"It's a fun exercise class," Mittens said. "You move around and make different shapes! They're called poses."

"Ok. I'll try it," said Dylan.

Dylan and Mittens entered the yoga studio and the class began.

All of this was very new
to Dylan. He had never
heard the names of all
these poses before.

And why was this one named
after a dog and not a cat?

Soon Dylan was able to try a pose named for cats, though.

"This is more like it," he thought.

As the class continued, it
seemed to get harder.

Dylan looked around and
noticed that all the other cats
knew exactly what to do, but
he felt unsure.

How did they remember all
those poses?

How?

When it came time to do the next pose, Dylan really wanted to try— it looked so cool! He wanted to be able to do it like all the others around him.

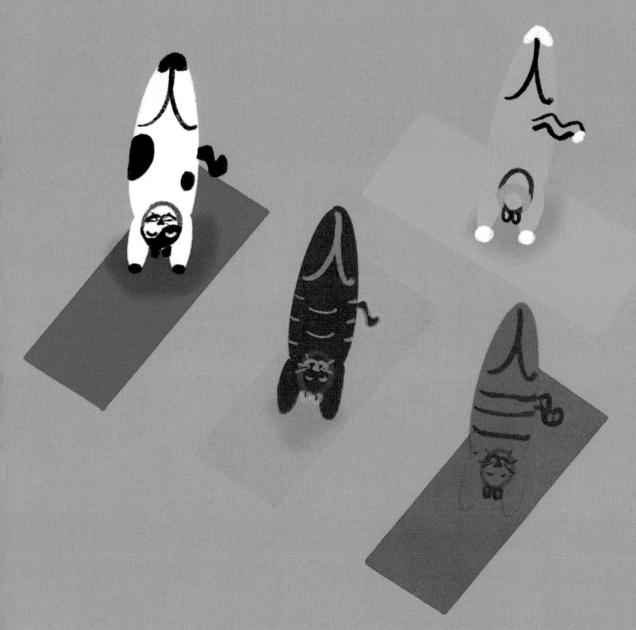

He thought, "I can do this!" as he
jumped into the pose.

But almost as soon as he
got up...

...he came tumbling down!

Dylan felt like crying.
He had tried the new pose,
but couldn't do it.

He started to wonder if he
could ever be as good as the
others. "Should I even try
anymore?" he thought.

What was the point if he
couldn't be good?

As Dylan sat on his mat, he thought back to the earlier part of class.

"I was able to do those poses," he said to himself. What if falling out of a pose didn't make him bad at yoga? What if it just meant that he was trying?

"If I keep practicing, maybe someday I'll be able to do that pose!" he thought.

Dylan got back up and decided to see what he was able to accomplish.

This time, he would do the poses in ways that worked for him, though. And he would see if he could just have fun.

For the rest of class Dylan followed along as best he could-

even if he looked a little different than the other cats.

He had lots of fun trying the many different poses, but his favorite was the last one where he got to lie down.

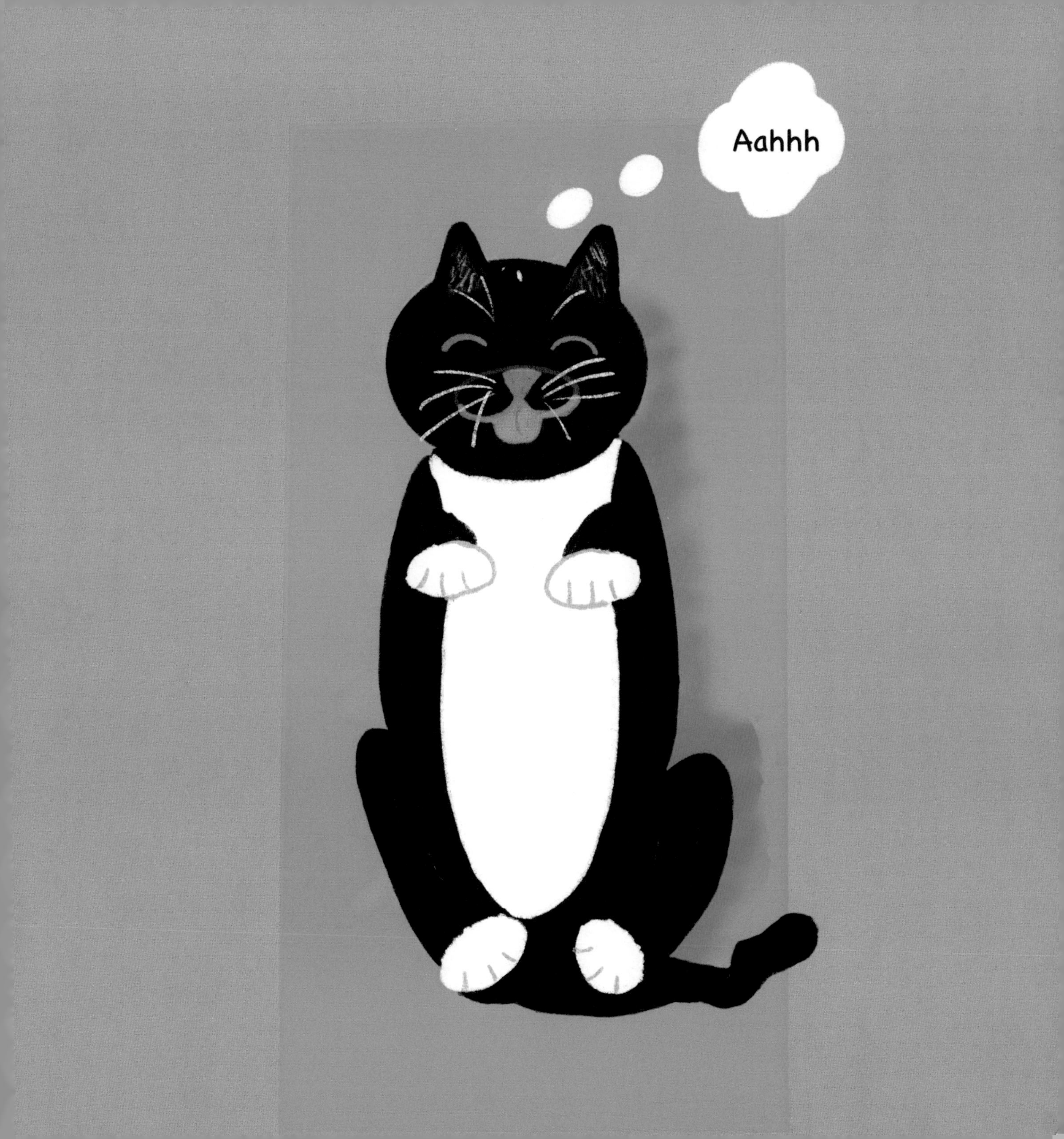
Aahhh

Later that night Dylan thought back to all the fun he'd had at his very first yoga class.

And he wondered, "What should I try next?"

Dylan Gunther

Dylan was adopted from a local animal shelter, and is four years old. When not being the inspiration for books, he enjoys napping, eating, and looking out the windows to patrol his neighborhood. He lives with his family in the
San Francisco Bay Area.

Kristin is thrilled to introduce the world to Dylan. When not working, you can find her reading, baking, and enjoying time with her family.

Made in the USA
Las Vegas, NV
19 January 2024

84631548R00021